Published by
Hogs Back Books
The Stables
Down Place
Hogs Back
Guildford GU3 1DE
www.hogsbackbooks.com

What? No bananas? is an adaptation by Karen Stevens and Hogs Back Books Ltd of original text and drawings of *Monkeys on a Fast* by Kaushik Viswanath and Shilpa Ranade

Monkeys on a Fast
© 2008 Karadi Tales Company Pvt Ltd (India)
All rights reserved
Original English edition published by Karadi Tales Company Pvt Ltd (India)
Adaptation rights arranged with Karadi Tales Company Pvt Ltd (India)

Printed in China
ISBN: 978-1-907432-06-4
British Library Cataloguing-in-Publication Data.
A catalogue record for this book is available from the British Library.
1 3 5 4 2

What? No Bananas?

Kaushik Viswanath ● Shilpa Ranade

Chakku, an old monkey chief, and his tribe
lived near a temple on the top of a hill.

he monkeys were greedy and lazy and spent the whole day eating bananas and sleeping on the branches of the banana trees.

One day, Bonno, the greediest and laziest monkey, ate far too many bananas (even for a greedy monkey). He settled down on his favourite branch, fell asleep and then

... fell out of the tree.

"That's it!" said Chakku, who had eaten one too many bananas himself that day. "It's time to turn over a new leaf."

Chakku gathered the tribe and said, "Tomorrow we will fast the whole day."

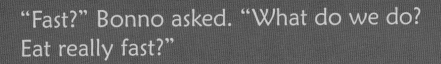

"Fast?" Bonno asked. "What do we do?
Eat really fast?"

All the monkeys laughed.

Chakku glared at them.

"A fast means not eating anything at all," he said.

The monkeys gasped.

"What? No bananas?" asked Bonno.

"No," replied Chakku. "Nothing."

"The whole day?" asked Bonno.

"Yes! The whole day," Chakku said. "Also, we will sit quietly and meditate so that we become calm, peaceful and clever monkeys."

The next day, Chakku led the monkeys to the temple terrace. He sat down, closed his eyes and began to meditate.

"Ommmmmmm ..." he said.

"Ommmmmmm ..." the monkeys repeated.

"Chief Chakku! Chief Chakku!"

Chakku opened his eyes to see Bonno shouting and waving his hand in the air. "I have an idea! Instead of meditating here in the hot sun, why don't we move closer to the banana trees? The leaves will give us shade."

Chakku thought about it and agreed.

The monkeys moved under the banana trees. Barely had they closed their eyes when Bonno spoke again.

"Chief Chakku! Chief Chakku!"

"What if we become so weak with hunger that by the end of the day we can't climb up the trees to reach the bananas? We could starve to death! Wouldn't it be better to sit at the top of the trees? That way, we'll be closer to the bananas when we end our fast."

Before Chakku had time to reply,
the monkeys had dashed up the trees.

hakku climbed after them.

Just as he reached the top, Bonno shouted,

I have a better idea. Why don't we pick a banana each and hold it in our hands? Who knows? By the end of the fast, we may not even have the strength to pick them off the tree."

The monkeys all grabbed a banana. One monkey thrust a banana into Chakku's hand too.

"Something's not right here," Chakku thought to himself as he held the lovely ripe fruit.

"Ommmmmmm…" he said,
determined to continue the meditation.

Imagine the monkey's delight when they
heard Bonno's voice again,

"Chief Chakku!

What if we become so drained of
energy that we can't peel the
bananas? Since we're going
to be holding the bananas,
why don't we peel them as
well?"

Before Chakku could disagree, the
monkeys had peeled the bananas.

"Let me peel it for you chief!" Bonno said, and he reached out for Chakku's banana. Chakku grabbed his hand away. He was not ready to give in.

"Ommmmmmm ..." he tried again. But it was useless. The smell of the ripe bananas was driving the monkeys mad.

"Chief Chakku!"

said Bonno. "Don't you think it would be a good idea just to take a bite or two out of our bananas? As long as we don't swallow them, we will still be fasting. Won't we?"

Chakku turned around to glare at Bonno, but found that all the monkeys had bitten into their bananas and were looking at him with their mouths full.

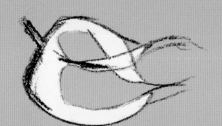

"Chief Chakku," Bonno
mumbled. "Does it make a difference if we store the bananas in our mouths or in our tummies? After all, they are all part of the same body."

"How true!" the monkeys agreed, and swallowed the bananas quickly.

And that was how the monkeys' fast ended.

Poor confused Chief Chakku couldn't work out how he'd been outwitted. He scratched his head, peeled his banana and ate it too.

The End